ated Rules of
FOOTBALL

By R. L. "Buddy" Patey
Illustrated by Patrick T. McRae

Ideals Children's Books • Nashville, Tennessee
an imprint of Hambleton-Hill Publishing, Inc.

For Mary who made my life, to Mark and Pat who have richly blessed my life, and to Madison and Hayden who are filling the evening of my life with sunshine!

In recognition of my mentors: George Gardner (SEC Supervisor), E.D. "Red" Cavette (SEC Referee), the late Cliff Norvell (SEC Umpire), and the late Webb Porter (TSSAA).

With special appreciation to my Ohio Valley Conference Football Officials, a truly unique group, and two great commissioners—Dan Beebe and Jim Delany.
—B.P.

For my wife, Marylee, who is always there when I need her.

Special thanks to Ryan McRae and Jared Stengel for their modeling expertise. Additional thanks to Troy Withington Photography.
—P.T.M.

Copyright © 1995 by Hambleton-Hill Publishing, Inc.

Published by Ideals Children's Books
An imprint of Hambleton-Hill Publishing, Inc.
Nashville, Tennessee 37218

Printed and bound in the United States of America

Library of Congress Cataloging-in-Publication Data
Patey, R. L.
    The illustrated rules of football / by R. L. "Buddy" Patey ; illustrated by Patrick T. McRae.
      p.   cm.
    Summary: Pictures and text explain the rules of football.
    ISBN 1-57102-049-7 (pbk)
    1. Football—United States—Rules—Juvenile literature. 2. National Football League—Juvenile literature. [1. Football—Rules.] I. McRae, Patrick, ill. II. Title.
GV955.P38   1995
796.332'02'022—dc20   95-8118
                                                          CIP
                                                          AC

Reviewed and endorsed by the National Federation of State High School Associations.

The National Federation was founded by educators dedicated to the development of young people through the medium of high school activities which are an integral part of the educational program.

The National Federation publishes rules in sixteen sports for high school competition and is pleased to endorse this football publication for youth.

For information about the National Federation football rules contact the National Federation at 11724 NW Plaza Circle, Kansas City, MO 64195.

Table of Contents

Note to Parents:

The Illustrated Rules of Football introduces young players to the basic rules of the game. Each rule is presented in simplified form and is accompanied by a detailed illustration for added clarity. Included is the information that is thought to be of most interest to young players. The fact-filled text and informative illustrations provide a basis for discussion of the game by players, coaches, and parents.

The author was an official in the SEC, where he served as Chief Umpire and was assigned to seven major bowl games. He currently serves as Supervisor of Officials for the Ohio Valley Conference and is Secretary of the NCAA Division I Football Supervisors. To write the rules in this book, he drew from his own experience, football tradition, and widely accepted rules used in various forms by virtually all football organizations.

It is the hope of the author and of the National Federation of State High School Associations that these rules will encourage good sportsmanship among players, coaches, and parents. In football, a winning attitude is just as important as a winning game.

So enjoy the game . . . and be a good sport!

The Game of Football

Although its ties go back to the games of rugby and soccer as played in Europe, football is truly "America's Game."

Football was invented by students and has always been known as the game of schools and colleges. As early as 1860, five high schools played the game on the famous Boston Common grounds. The first college game was played in 1869 between student teams from Princeton and Rutgers. Today football is played by athletes from elementary school all the way up to the professional teams of the National Football League (NFL).

Television has made football the most popular of all American sports, and many college and professional games can be seen each week during the season. After the season, fans can see nineteen bowl games matching college teams from all over the nation. Then they can watch the Super Bowl, which determines the NFL champion.

The object of the game is simple. One team tries to get the ball over the opponent's goal line by either running with the ball or passing the ball. Good sportsmanship is a most important part of the game of football. Players should have good attitudes, play by the rules, and respect their opponents and the officials—no matter who is winning.

The Rules of the Game

Rule 1: The Field of Play

The **field of play** is in the shape of a rectangle. It is 120 yards (360 feet) long and 53 1/3 yards (160 feet) wide.

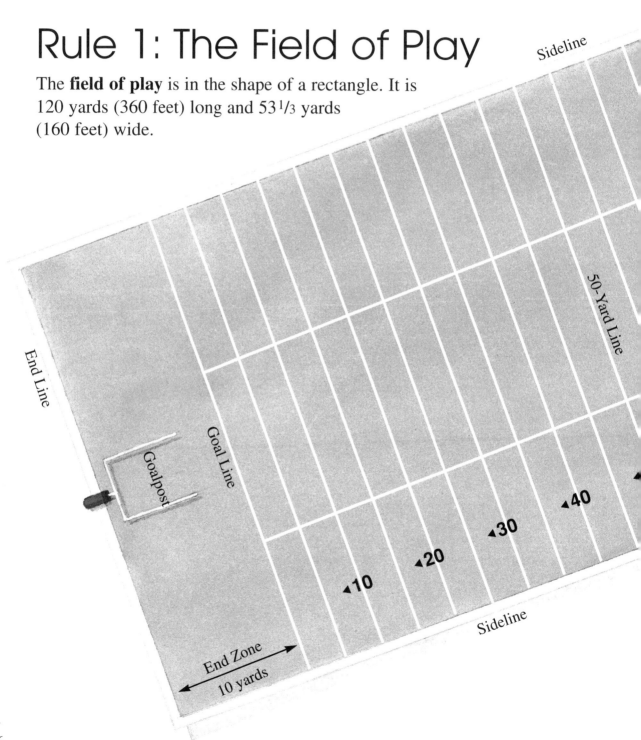

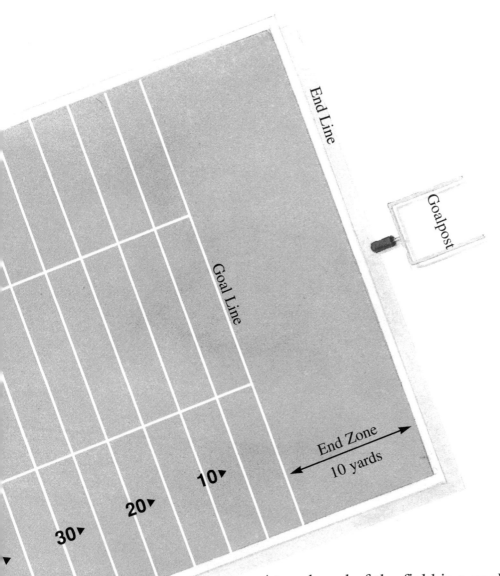

At each end of the field is a **goal line**. This is the line that each team defends from its opponents. The goal line is 4 inches wide and reaches from sideline to sideline. If a player crosses the opponent's goal line with the ball, a touchdown is scored.

The **end zone** is the 10-yard area from the goal line to the end line. A touchdown is scored if a player carries the ball or catches a pass inside the opposing team's end zone.

The **50-yard line** separates the field into halves. Each half is marked off with **yard lines** every 5 yards.

The **sidelines** and **end lines** are the boundary lines which determine if the ball or a player is out-of-bounds.

Rule 2: The Ball

The **football** is tan in color. It is made of pebbled leather or rubber with 1-inch white stripes across the top two panels. On the top seam are eight equally spaced laces.

The ball is approximately 11 inches long. The short circumference (the distance around the center of the ball) is generally 21 inches and the long circumference is 28 inches. A smaller ball is sometimes used by youth and middle school leagues.

Rule 3: The Goalposts

The **goalpost** is used in scoring field goals and extra points (see Rule 8). There is one goalpost at each end of the field. It is located on the end line and halfway between the sidelines.

The goalpost has either one or two **base posts**, a **crossbar**, and two **uprights** extending above the crossbar. The crossbar must be 10 feet from the ground. For youth and high school games, the crossbar must be 23 feet 4 inches wide, but for college and professional games, it must be 18 feet 6 inches wide. The uprights must reach at least 10 feet above the crossbar for youth teams, 20 feet for college, and 30 feet for professional.

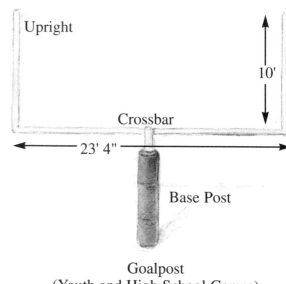

Upright

10'

Crossbar

23' 4"

Base Post

Goalpost
(Youth and High School Games)

Yardage Chain

Down Marker

Rule 4: Yardage Chain and Down Marker

The **yardage chain** is used to show how far the offensive team has moved the ball since the first down (see Rule 12). The yardage chain is exactly 10 yards long, and it joins two rods. The back rod is placed on the sideline at a spot even with the front point of the football at the first down. The front rod is used to show where the ball must be moved to in order to get a new series of four downs.

The **down marker** is another rod which holds panels labeled 1, 2, 3, and 4. These panels are used to show whether it is the first, second, third, or fourth down.

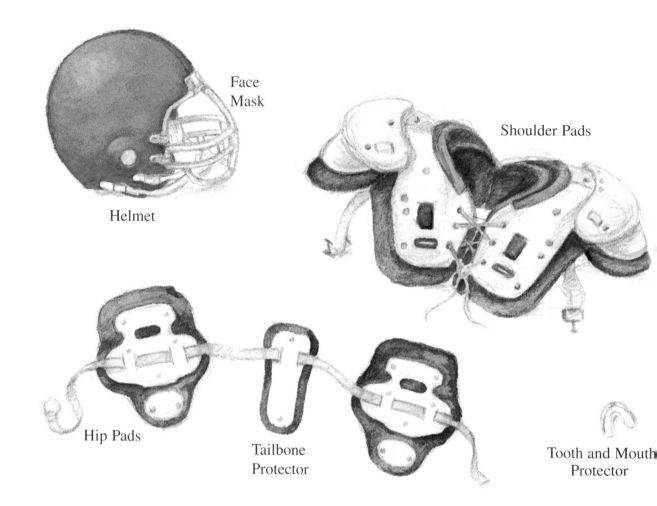

Face Mask

Shoulder Pads

Helmet

Hip Pads

Tailbone Protector

Tooth and Mouth Protector

Rule 5: Required Player Equipment

Each player must wear the following equipment: helmet, face mask, hip pads with a tailbone protector, a jersey with a number from 1 to 99 (on the front and back), kneepads, pants which cover the knees and kneepads, shoulder pads, thigh pads, and a tooth and mouth protector. An athletic cup is recommended for young players.

College players are not required to wear shoes, but most players choose to wear them. Kickers, however, often prefer to kick barefoot. High school and NFL players must wear shoes, although barefoot kicking is sometimes allowed in the NFL.

Jersey

Thigh Pads

Socks

Kneepads

Shoes

Pants

11

Rule 6: The Officials

An official's job is to enforce the rules of the game. An official throws a gold flag when a foul is called and blows a whistle to declare that the ball is dead and the play is over.

The **referee** is the head official and has the final word on all rulings. Other officials who may assist the referee include the umpire, linesman, line judge, side judge, field judge, and back judge.

Depending on the age and skill level of the teams involved, there may be from three to seven officials in a football game. Youth games usually have three officials, middle schools and high schools have four or five, colleges have from five to seven, and professional games have seven.

Referee

Umpire
(And Other Officials)

Rule 7: Game Time

The game time is divided into two halves. Each **half** is divided into two **quarters**, so that a game has four quarters. Quarters may last from 8 to 15 minutes. For youth leagues, each quarter generally lasts 8 minutes.

Halftime is the break between the first and second halves. It can last from 10 to 20 minutes, but it is usually 15 minutes for youth games. There is also a 1-minute break between the first and second quarters and between the third and fourth quarters.

When a game is tied at the end of regular play, some leagues play extra periods, or **overtimes**, until there is a winner.

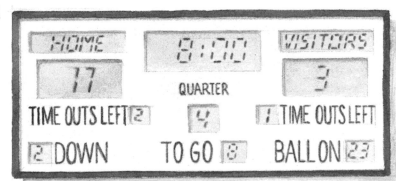

Rule 8: Scoring

A team scores by making a touchdown, extra point, field goal, or safety.

A **touchdown** counts 6 points. To score a touchdown, a player must carry the ball across the opponent's goal line or catch a pass in the opponent's end zone. As long as any part of the football touches on or above the goal line, a touchdown is scored.

After a touchdown, a team may try to win **extra points** from the 3-yard line. If the ball is kicked between the uprights of the opponent's goalpost, 1 point is scored. If the ball is carried or passed across the opponent's goal line, 2 points are scored.

A **field goal** counts 3 points. To score a field goal, the ball must be kicked between the uprights of the opponent's goalpost.

If a player is downed, or tackled, in his own team's end zone with the ball, it is called a **safety**. The opposing team is awarded 2 points.

Rule 9: The Captain

As many as four captains from each team may come to the center of the field for the coin toss (see Rule 11). Once the game begins, each team may have only one captain. The **captain** speaks for the team in all matters with the officials.

Rule 10: The Teams

Each team has eleven players on the playing field at one time. Substitute players may enter the game any time that a play is not in progress, without reporting to any official.

The team that puts the ball into play with a snap is called the **offense** and the other team is the **defense**. The team that puts the ball into play with a kickoff may be called the **kicking team**, while the other team is called the **receiving team**.

At the beginning of each down, or play, the two teams face each other at the line of scrimmage. The offensive team has seven players on its line of scrimmage: a center, two guards, two tackles, and two ends. In the **offensive backfield**, or area behind the line of scrimmage, there are usually a quarterback, a fullback, and two halfbacks.

The defensive team usually has from four to seven players, called linemen, on its line of scrimmage. The remaining defensive players, called linebackers or pass defenders, are behind the linemen. (See pages 22–27 for more information on players' positions.)

Offense

QB	quarterback
HB	halfback
FB	fullback
E	end
C	center
G	guard
T	tackle

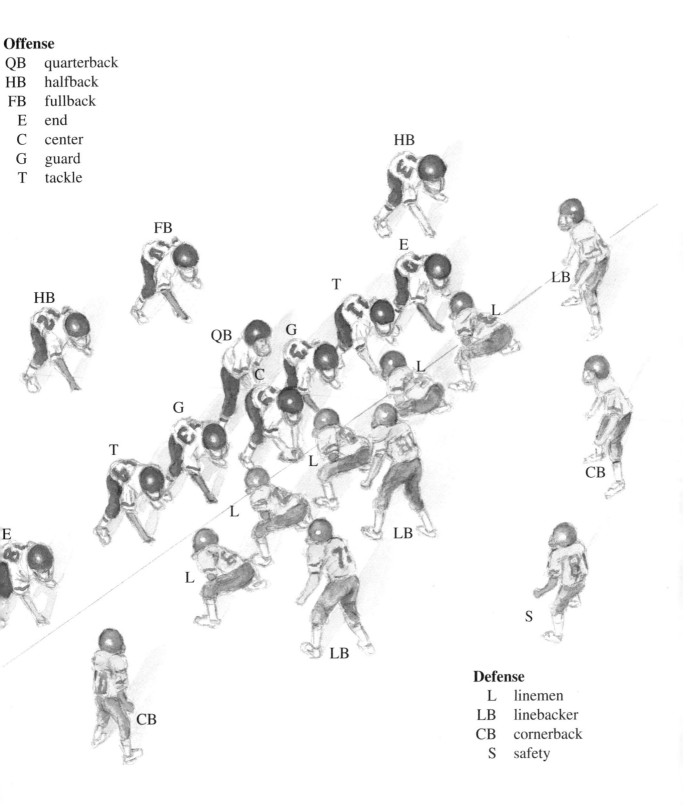

HB

FB

E

HB

T

QB

G

G

C

L

LB

L

L

T

L

E

L

LB

L

CB

LB

S

CB

Defense

L	linemen
LB	linebacker
CB	cornerback
S	safety

15

Rule 11: Starting the Game

To begin the game, the team captains meet at the center of the 50-yard line. The referee tosses a coin, and the visiting team calls "heads" or "tails." The winner of the toss may have first choice to make the kickoff or receive the kickoff, or he may choose the goal his team will defend. The loser of the toss will have the same choices at the beginning of the second half. In some leagues, the winner of the toss may delay having "first choice" till the beginning of the second half.

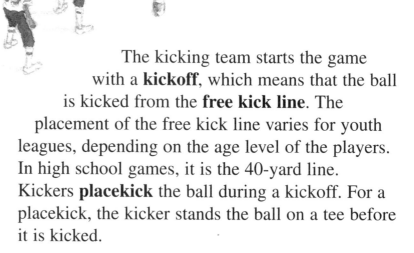

The kicking team starts the game with a **kickoff**, which means that the ball is kicked from the **free kick line**. The placement of the free kick line varies for youth leagues, depending on the age level of the players. In high school games, it is the 40-yard line. Kickers **placekick** the ball during a kickoff. For a placekick, the kicker stands the ball on a tee before it is kicked.

Rule 12:
Putting the Ball into Play

After the kickoff, the two teams line up facing each other at the line of scrimmage. The center for the receiving, or offensive, team will put the ball into play by snapping the ball from its place on the ground back to the quarterback. The quarterback will either run with the ball, pass it, or hand it off to another backfield player.

The offensive team has four **downs**, or tries (also called plays), to gain 10 yards. If they gain 10 yards or more before they use all four downs, they get a **first down** and four more chances to gain another 10 yards. This continues until they fail to gain 10 yards in four downs, score, or lose the ball by a fumble or pass interception. Usually if a team has not gained 10 yards after the third down, they will **punt** the ball to the other team on the fourth down. For a punt, the kicker drops the ball and kicks it before it hits the ground.

After a field goal, or after a touchdown and extra point attempt, the ball is put back into play with a kickoff by the team that scored. After a safety, the team that was scored against kicks the ball from their 20-yard line, and it may be a punt or a placekick.

Rule 13: Formations

When the offense is putting the ball into play, there must be at least seven offensive players on the line of scrimmage. The defensive players may be placed anywhere on or behind the line of scrimmage. (For an explanation of players' positions, see pages 22–27.)

There are many different offensive **formations**, or ways of arranging the offensive players. The offensive team places seven players called linemen at the line of scrimmage, usually with three on each side of the center. The remaining players are placed in the backfield. The T-formation, I-formation, wishbone formation, and punt formation are some of the most popular offensive formations.

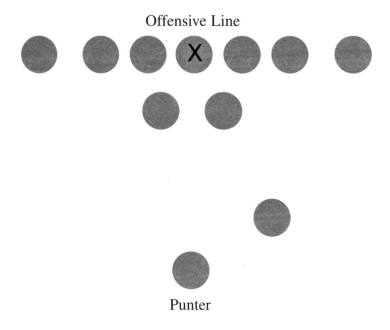

Offensive Line

Punter

Punt Formation: The punter is about 12 yards deep, behind the line of scrimmage. The other backfield players are located in positions to block for the punter.

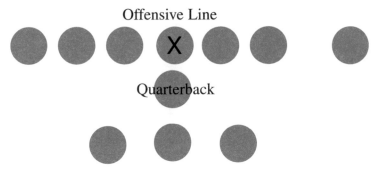

T-Formation: The quarterback is crouched behind the center to receive the snap. One backfield player is behind the quarterback, and there is another player on each side of this backfield player.

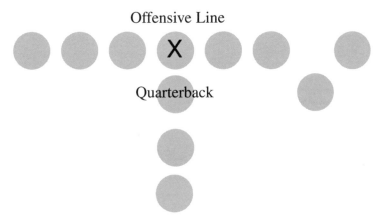

I-Formation: The quarterback is crouched to receive the snap. Two or three backfield players are positioned in a straight line behind the quarterback.

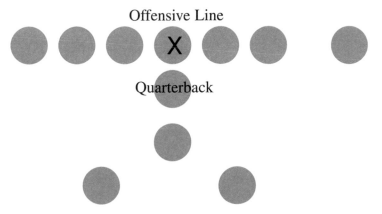

Wishbone Formation: The backfield players are set in positions that resemble a wishbone. The quarterback is behind the center, and one backfield player is behind the quarterback. The other two players are on each side of the first backfield player and about a yard deeper.

Rule 14: Out-of-Bounds

A player is **out-of-bounds** if he touches the ground on or outside the boundary lines, or if he touches anything that is on or outside these lines, other than another player or an official.

A ball that is not in a player's possession is out-of-bounds if it touches anything that is on or outside the boundary lines.

Rule 15: Fouls

A **foul** is any breaking of the rules. If a player commits a foul, his team may be penalized with the loss of yardage, the loss of the down, or both. The following are some common fouls.

1. **Delay of Game:** After the referee blows the whistle and signals to begin play, the offense has 25 seconds to put the ball into play. If more time is taken, it is a foul.

2. **Holding:** No player can grasp or clamp his arms around an opponent unless the opponent has the ball.

3. **Personal Foul:** No player can kick an opponent or strike an opponent with a fist, forearm, hand, head, or knee. Tripping is a foul, unless it is used to bring down the player who has the ball. Other personal fouls are roughing, contacting an opponent after the ball is dead, and contacting an opponent who is obviously out of play.

4. **Face Mask:** A player cannot grasp another's face mask or helmet.

5. **Roughing:** A defensive player cannot run into a kicker who has his kicking foot off the ground, nor can he run into the player who is holding the ball for a placekick. A defensive player must also try to avoid running into a passer after the ball has left the passer's hand.

6. **Interference:** A defensive player cannot interfere with a receiver who is trying to catch a pass or a kick by contacting him before he touches the ball.

7. **Clipping:** A player cannot block or push an opponent in the back. Blocking below the waist from any direction is also a foul.

8. **Illegal Shift:** If one or more players (in high school or youth games) moves to a new position after the team is set at the line of scrimmage, he (or they) must be motionless for at least 1 second before the snap; if not, it is called an illegal shift.

9. **Unsportsmanlike Conduct:** No player shall make derogatory remarks, use profanity, or make taunting actions.

The Players

The Linemen

There are seven **offensive linemen**: the **center**, two **guards**, two **tackles**, and two **ends**. The center is set in the middle of the line of scrimmage. The guards line up so that one is on each side of the center, with a tackle beside each guard and an end beside each tackle.

The center is the player who snaps the ball back to the quarterback or punter. The guards, tackles, and ends block the defensive team's players. They try to open up holes for the runners and protect the passer, who is usually the quarterback. Offensive linemen wear a number from 50 through 79 on their jerseys.

Usually there are from five to seven **defensive linemen**. Their job is to tackle the runner and to prevent him from gaining yardage. They also try to get to the quarterback and tackle him before he can pass the ball or hand it off. Defensive linemen can wear any number on their jersey, but they usually wear a number from 50 through 79.

Center in Set
Position

End in One Type of Set Position (Set Position for an End May Also Be an Upright Stance)

Center, Guard, Tackle, or End (Blocking)

Guard or Tackle in Set Position

The Backfield Players

The **offensive backfield players** are the quarterback, the fullback, and two halfbacks. They wear a number from 1 through 49 on their jerseys.

The **quarterback** calls the plays in the huddle before each down. At the line of scrimmage, he crouches behind the center to receive the snap. The quarterback then hands the ball off to another player, passes it, or runs with it himself.

The **fullback** and **halfbacks** run the ball, catch passes, block for the runner when they do not have the ball, and block to protect the passer.

The **defensive backfield players** form the last line of defense against the offense. They try to prevent the offense from gaining yardage by running the ball and completing passes. Defensive backfield players usually wear a number from 1 through 49 or from 80 through 99.

The **cornerback** is the defensive backfield player whose position is usually wider and somewhat deeper than the linebackers, but not as deep as the safety.

The **safety** is the defensive backfield player whose position is deepest in the formation. (This "safety" is, of course, different from the safety described in Rule 8.)

The Pass Receivers

Offensive **pass receivers** may be placed on the end of the line of scrimmage or in the offensive backfield. Their job is to get into the open and catch passes for big yardage gains. Pass receivers must wear a number from 1 through 49 or from 80 through 99. They are also called ends, wide receivers, or wideouts.

The Linebackers

The **linebackers** are placed 2 to 5 yards behind the defensive linemen in a formation. Their job is to keep the offensive runners from gaining yardage and to defend against short passes. Linebackers can wear any number on their jersey, but they usually wear a number from 50 through 79.

The Kicker

The **kicker** is the player who kicks the ball for the field goals, extra points, kickoffs, and punts.

27

Important Signals

Ball Ready for Play
Starts 25-second count during which ball must be put in play

Touchdown, Field Goal, or **Points after a Touchdown**

Safety

Interference

Intentional Grounding
Ball has been thrown into an area where there is no eligible receiver to try to prevent a loss of yardage

Holding

Face Mask

Personal Foul

Roughing the Kicker

Clipping

Sportsmanship in the Game of Football

Sportsmanship and teamwork go hand in hand. The players who work together and sacrifice being stars for the good of the team are showing good sportsmanship.

Football teaches the lessons of fair play—doing your best even when you are losing and respecting your teammates, your opponents, and the officials. A good player works hard to win, but if he loses, he congratulates his opponents for their winning effort. When a player who has learned good sportsmanship wins, he also congratulates his opponents for their hard play; and he accepts congratulations with appreciation and a humble attitude.

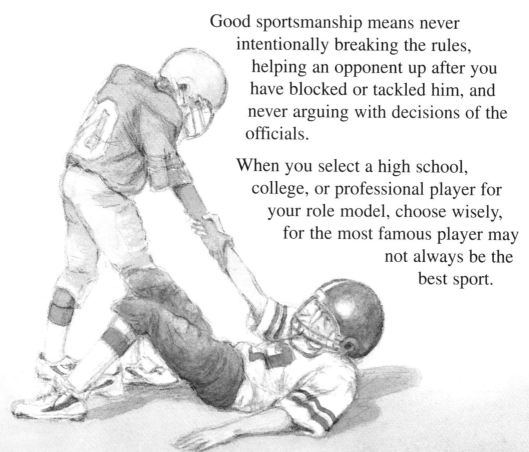

Good sportsmanship means never intentionally breaking the rules, helping an opponent up after you have blocked or tackled him, and never arguing with decisions of the officials.

When you select a high school, college, or professional player for your role model, choose wisely, for the most famous player may not always be the best sport.

Summary of the Rules of Football

Rule 1: The Field of Play
The football field is in the shape of a rectangle. It is 120 yards (360 feet) long and 53$\frac{1}{3}$ yards (160 feet) wide. The field is marked off with yard lines every 5 yards. At each end of the field is a goal line. The sidelines and end lines are the boundary lines which determine if a player or the ball is out-of-bounds.

Rule 2: The Ball
The football is tan in color and is made of pebbled leather or rubber. It is approximately 11 inches long. The short circumference is about 21 inches, and the long circumference is 28 inches.

Rule 3: The Goalposts
The goalpost is used in scoring field goals and extra points. There is one goalpost at each end of the field.

Rule 4: Yardage Chain and Down Marker
The yardage chain is used to show how far the offensive team has moved the ball since the first down. The down marker is used to show whether it is the first, second, third, or fourth down.

Rule 5: Required Player Equipment
Each player must wear the following equipment: helmet, face mask, hip pads with a tailbone protector, jersey, kneepads, pants which cover the knees and kneepads, shoulder pads, thigh pads, and a tooth and mouth protector.

Rule 6: The Officials
An official's job is to enforce the rules of the game. The referee is the head official and has the final word on all rulings. There may be from three to seven officials in a game.

Rule 7: Game Time
The game time is divided into two halves. Each half is divided into two quarters, so that a game has four quarters. Halftime is the break between the first and second halves. There is also a 1-minute break between the first and second quarters and between the third and fourth quarters.

Rule 8: Scoring
A team scores points by making a touchdown, extra point, field goal, or safety.

Rule 9: The Captain
The captain speaks for the team in all matters with the officials.

Rule 10: The Teams
Each team has eleven players on the field at one time. The team that puts the ball into play with a snap is called the offense and the other team is the defense. The team that puts the ball into play with a kickoff is the kicking team and the other team is the receiving team.

Rule 11: Starting the Game
A coin toss determines which team will kick the ball, which team will receive the kickoff, and which goal each team will defend. The kicking team starts the game with a kickoff.

Rule 12: Putting the Ball into Play
After the kickoff, the two teams line up facing each other at the line of scrimmage. The offensive team will put the ball into play by snapping the ball from its place on the ground to the quarterback. After a touchdown, extra point attempt, or field goal, the ball is put into play with a kickoff by the team that scored.

Rule 13: Formations
When the offense is putting the ball into play, there must be at least seven offensive players on the line of scrimmage. Defensive players may be placed anywhere on or behind the line of scrimmage.

Rule 14: Out-of-Bounds
A player is out-of-bounds if he touches anything on or outside the boundary lines except another player or an official. A ball is out-of-bounds if it touches anything on or outside the boundary lines.

Rule 15: Fouls
A foul is any breaking of the rules. If a player commits a foul, his team may be penalized with the loss of yardage, the loss of a down, or both.

Vocabulary of the Game

block: to contact an opponent with any part of the body

defensive backfield: area behind the defensive linemen; OR the players behind the defensive linemen

fumble: when a player loses possession of the ball, except when the ball is passed or kicked

hand off: to transfer the ball from one player's hands to the hands of a teammate

huddle: to group together to call the plays; OR the group itself

interception: when an opponent catches any pass or fumble

line of scrimmage: imaginary line running through each end of the ball that determines how the teams will line up before a play; the position of the line of scrimmage is based on where the ball is placed by the officials following each play

live ball: during a down, a ball that is in the possession of a player or is loose from a pass, kick, or fumble (such a ball is said to be **in play**)

offensive backfield: area behind the offensive linemen; OR the players behind the offensive linemen

open up holes: to block opponents in order to make an opening for the runner

play: the action following the snap or kickoff

shift: when two or more offensive players move from one position to another position

snap: the center hands the ball back between his legs to the quarterback or passes it back to another backfield player or to the punter

yardage: number of yards gained or lost during a play

1135